No Longer Alone:
Springtrap

Two Sovereigns Publishing

Table of Contents

CHAPTER I

Children…My god…Still alive? No…you can't be! You're…you're…dead…oh God, you're dead. Ghosts! You're…ghosts…?

"Go away, go away! Leave me alone! I'm sorry…so sorry…it's just my nature, my addiction, I n-need help…I'm…sorry…I took your lives just to excite mine…I see that now! I see that I did wrong…go away, I see the sins, I see them! Please, just go away, go away!"

I must hide…but where? Where? A gold suit…a rabbit suit…I didn't read the…manual…it's faulty apparently…I ignore it…I disregard the warning sign above it, it seems fine…I'll wear that, I'll hide in it…looks like a piece of equipment…

Tight…very tight…fitting. The ghosts can't find me. They are looking and they can't find me!

"If I could take back what I did, I would. If I could go back in time to stop myself I would! Please don't find me…please…"

Pain…now I'm feeling pain, why? Why am I feeling pain…wait, metal robs are…s-sticking into me, joints are tightening around me, I'm…I'm being c-crushed! Oh god, oh shit! It hurts, oh god, it hurts!

"Somebody help me!"

The dead children just…stare at me…they watch me. Smiling…they're smiling.

I feel my bones break, my flesh being ripped and my warm blood drenching me from every ripped hole. The last sounds I hear is my skull cracking through squashed pressure and my blood gurgled scream…darkness…nothing.

30 Years later

The first things I remember is the smell of rotten meat - that stench will live with me forever. My nostrils flared and I jolted myself awake. I gasp and scream in panic, waving my arms about to rid of the ghosts that were following me…only, there were no ghosts, I was just slashing out at thin air…it took me a while to realize where I was…I was at Freddy Fazbear's pizza emporium, I was the night guard…was I dreaming? Did I fall asleep…? Yeah, I must've done.

"Crap, sleeping on the job!"- I yelled. The first thing I did was to look at my watch but instead I saw something unnerving…a grey yellow wrist that was tatty and dirty, as if the colour had died over time…dried blood was stained all over me…I then looked at my hands, thick monstrous hands, I moved my fingers, I managed to wiggle them…it then occurred to me that I was wearing the costume I'd snuck into…the golden rabbit suit, the faulty one…

"Oh no…" I gasped…

That pain was coming back to me…the sound of my skull being crushed…it was all to real.

Denial hit me next, there was no way this was real. I moved my feet…dirty yellow joints creaked and clanked, it was strange though…the suit didn't feel heavier than it did when I put it on. As my senses were coming back to me, I took advantage of this and pushed myself up…I wobbled at first, almost falling on my backside, but soon I got the right balance. My joints were stiff, but, to my relief, I was able to move. Still, it felt like years since I did…only a matter of time before I find that truth out…

I was in a different place but I didn't clock onto this just yet, I needed to find a mirror. The only place I knew was the gent's toilets, so I proceeded to go to it. I walked down a corridor but…it wasn't the same corridor…something about this place was different…it seemed like a pizza parlour but it was all worn and wasted, dust everywhere, cob webs filling all the corners and covering objects and boxes…as I proceed down what I perceived to be the pizza parlour, I decided to keep the questions to myself and find answers. But I needed to see what I looked like…of course, it still didn't stop me thinking about the questions:

Am I dead?

Am I still dreaming?

Did I get sacked?

Am I in jail…?

Did they find the children's bodies?

A few feet down the corridor and it suddenly became unfamiliar…I swear to God the men's toilets were on the left hand side, I swear blindly by it…but no door. There was a door on the right, which I quickly peeked my head through but all I could see was a few run down arcades; it was a dead end in there. I sighed but was getting frustrated…any form of reflection would do now. So I carried on down the corridor, I was coming up to a few doors now; none had signs on them though…what is this place? I shrugged and opened the first one…

"Hello! Hello?" I cried out. Not a soul, not a single bit of noise. The place was dead. I turned to see a Foxy head on the wall, it had a light glowing from it but on closer inspection it was an original Foxy head…it was rather weird to look at, I was half expecting it to jump out on me or force me into a nervous jump scare. I looked around…the light was dim but my vision was surprisingly good. It was clear that this place had people in it at some point…everything was pushed against the wall and I noticed Freddy Fazbear merchandise, cups, T-Shirts plushes and the stupid music box, yeah the whole lot. It was a mess but organized mess…but still, everything was different…there was no way that this was Freddy Fazbears pizza emporium but…a replica, maybe? Yet, another truth I'd soon learn about.

I did come across a mirror eventually, but it was broken into pieces, it didn't matter, one little shard would be enough, so I picked up the biggest piece and stared right into it…

I gasped in horror…almost dropping the piece. In front of me was a horrific looking mascot, tattered, dirty, worn and ripped at some point, with bits of dried blood all over me, the face was worse, it was like my face was stitched together…my eyes were glowing to a degree…but I was still in the suit and yet, I couldn't get out. It felt like it was a part of me. It wasn't as heavy when I put it on…I felt my face, I could feel every texture, the grimy suede over my face…at first I thought I was dreaming again, no…a nightmare, but a nightmare all too real…I could move my jaw and so would the suit's jaw…it was…attached to me as well…I was the suit…I AM the suit.

When I opened my jaw again, I could see something inside…something brown, almost like a brownish red colour…my hands were shaking, I opened my mouth wider and in the reflection, I could see a rotten face…it had no eyes, it's jaw open as well, most of the teeth fallen out, a skull like head, dried up skin, cracking as I move…a lump of dried skin fell out of my mouth, oddly enough this made me gag.

Oh God…it was…it's me…

"What is this shit?" I cried. "What is going on…?"

How am I still alive if my body is…trapped in this suit…how?

The shock lasted for some time…I was in the suit, my body dead and yet…here I am. I was…SPRINGTRAP…This is impossible…

Answers would come to me sooner…but, I needed help, I was confused, scared, helpless, puzzled and perplexed…no one about to help me, no one to aid me through this hell…This place was abandoned. Clearly, it hasn't been used in years, where the hell am I? No one could answer these questions for me; for there was not a soul in sight…I was alone…

This is my punishment…I deserve this…
And yet, I don't want to be alone…

CHAPTER II

Springtrap couldn't believe he was alive – it still didn't sink in. He wanted help but no one could help him, not a soul. He wanted to find clues of the timeline he was "living in" and any possible answers he could find. He checked nearly every room but each one just looked the same, all dusty, unusable, messy…empty. Sure, he found the kitchen and small diner that didn't even look real but nothing that could be useful to him…he didn't even feel hungry. Was it because he was in shock or had his body terminated any natural sources he could do with? His breathing was strangely normal, though it felt like he wasn't breathing at times…the only thing he still had was his feelings, his emotions…but he knew nothing else but sadness and confusion.

He came to another door called the maintenance room, he grabbed the handle and tried to open it but it wouldn't budge, it was obviously locked…or perhaps something was blocking it? But most likely locked. He sighed…as he continued walking. It was starting to come together; this place wasn't the pizza emporium where he worked but some sort of…replica. It was like a history of Freddy Fazbear but instead of looking fun it seemed more adult or least, not for younger kids…it was made as an attraction, at least judging by the leaflets he had found, scattered all over the place. It still wasn't coming together though. Was his workplace knocked down and this was built in place...or was he moved here?

Suddenly, another question popped in his head: Did they notice I was trapped in this suit? Did they just…leave me and dump me here? Come on, Vince, think for Christ sake, think! Then again…surely they noticed the blood…this doesn't make sense…

Springtrap was walking along a corridor and noticed some paper clippings on the wall. He only took quick glances but one caught his eye, a clipping about missing children. He took it off the wall to get a better look, just a snippet but he read it…

-- TWO CHILDREN MISSING.

Two children, Frank, age 6 and Christine, age 7 have not been seen since the late hours on Sunday evening. It has been two days now and the police suspect foul play. The parents of the two are condemning the police for not searching earlier and are asking anyone if they had seen anything. One man has been questioned--

Springtrap sighed…he remembered being questioned but lied convincingly.

He noticed another snippet on the wall, again he took it down to read.

--ACCIDENT AT FREDDY FAZgfjfgdfgj (The headline was worn out)

An unnamed boy for legal reasons, aged 8 has been sent to hospital due to an accident at the family diner, the world famous (Missing font) frontal..lobe… that caused serious injury, though paramedical were baffled how the child managed to climb onto an animatronic and get his head wedge between the heavy duty moving mouth parts. The child's older broth--

Springtrap didn't want to read any more…a tear slowly dripped from his eye socket.

SPRINGTRAP: You didn't w-wake up…

The yellow rabbit dropped the piece of paper and fell to his knees, he started sobbing some more before putting his head in his hands.

SPRINGTRAP: (*crying*) I'm sorry…oh God forgive me…I'm sorry…

That was just the start, wasn't it? You just stared at him…you watched him flap like a fish out of water, he struggled…he wanted you to stop…he was helpless…he was scared…but you and your damn friends just watched him…watched him suffer…you watched his skull squeeze like you would with juice from an orange…you smiled…you freaking smiled!

SPRINGTRAP: I'm sorry!

No…you are not! How can you be sorry…when you made others suffer, almost the same fate! How can you show remorse now!

Springtrap was shaking his head, the voices in his head were ringing true, like they echoed throughout the room. He stood up and ran as if to escape the voices.

MAY. YOU. SUFFER!

Springtrap came to a room, it was a security office. He grabbed the hand and shook it violently, trying to get in the room…his sadness became frustrating and he shoulder barged the door. It was no use but his anger upped his strength and kicked the door down, the lock breaking and flying off. He ran into the room, grabbing the nearest thing, which was a swivel chair and chucked it across the room, smashing into a glass window, though only creating a wed like crack over the window. He kicked and punched boxes…until his anger was released, he calmed down, his breathing was heavy but then his throat grew sore as he tried to hold back his tears…but he couldn't…as the image of his brother came back to him. The scream…that…scream…and then silence.

SPRINGTRAP: How can I take it back…?

VOICE: You…can't…

Springtrap turned around but nobody was there, only a box full of animatronic spare heads. Springtrap sighed but then the voice arose again.

VOICE: How does it feel?

He turned around again and stared at the box again only to be in complete shock of see some glowing eyes coming from a Freddy Fazbear head. The head was grinning.

FREDDY: How does it feel to kill your brother?

SPRINGTRAP: No, this is…this is not happening…?

FREDDY: *(grins)*In your head, I AM happening! Couldn't contain your thoughts so you bring me to life…in your pathetic little mind…

SPRINGTRAP: In my…head?

FREDDY: Yes…

SPRINGTRAP: Then go away…Get out of my head!

FREDDY: You killed him! Your own brother, you killed him! Murderer!

SPRINGTRAP: I'm sorry!

Then the other glowed too. Springtrap backed up onto a monitor, trying to get away. It was all in his head but it felt all too real.

BONNIE: You're a scum! You killed for fun! You killed innocent children!

CHICA: why did you get to live? Why did the children have to die?

FREDDY: You haven't had justice. This "suit" is just a prison but you still have yet to pay the PRICE!

SPRINGTRAP: LEAVE ME ALONE! I BEG OF YOU!

FREDDY: You'll always…be alone…forever!

Springtrap screamed, he then ran towards the box and kicked the contents out, the lights in the eyes disappeared like turning of a switch. He smashed the Freddy head with his fist, he stamped on Bonnie's head, breaking it with ease and then he chucked Chica's head onto the control panel. This activated something, as suddenly all the lights started to come on, some struggled and flickered and then the monitor came on, static at first but became clearer. Springtrap looked at the screen, they seem to have some sort of night vision as the room could easily be seen; though, now and then, the static would interfere.

It was an old system, as it buzzed, he figured there was loose wiring. But this place was old, he was surprised it still worked. He looked at the control panel and pressed numerous buttons, some didn't do much…one strangely had a sound of a child laughing mischievously. He eventually found a button that would change the camera's view and one swapping from room to room…if only he found this earlier. He flipped through the cameras, nothing except dimmed lit rooms and the Foxy head he'd seen earlier.

He flipped through the channels quickly and at a glimpse…saw a figure standing in the background. Springtrap took a double take and went back to the room where he saw a figure…but the shadow or whatever it was, was gone. Springtrap blinked. He definitely saw something there…in the corridor, near the maintenance room. And he swore that the door to the maintenance was now open. Springtrap rubbed his eyes, taking his glance off the screen. He figured that his mind had been playing tricks on him. Just then he heard a slam, coming from the corridor. He looked up and the door was now locked…he gasped as he took steps back. This wasn't his mind playing tricks…there is definitely someone here with him. Whoever it is, they have locked themselves away. Springtrap took a deep breath, he then flipped through the channels till he could get to the maintenance room…but it was blank, dark…the lights were out.

SPRINGTRAP**:** Oh shit…what is in there?

Springtrap couldn't decide whether this was a good thing that someone was here with him, as he really needed to talk to someone. Being isolated made him feel vulnerable but…maybe…just maybe this was a chance to speak to someone, someone real…and not just with his mind. He bit his lip and decided to go investigate. He wasn't sure of what he'd find…

CHAPTER III

Springtrap just stood at the door of the maintenance room, looking at the dirty metal sign. Something was behind that door, something real…he reached out his hand to touch the door handle but his hand started to shake…he couldn't understand it, he never felt fear of curiosity before, so why should this be different…maybe it's because what he saw wasn't quite human, judging by the shadow…at least a quick glimpse of it, it was missing a hand. Springtrap tried to pull himself together; he gritted his teeth in frustration…and took a deep breath.

SPRINGTRAP**:** Come on, damn it, come on…it's just a door, it's just a stupid door…

Though his mind would go back to thinking what was behind the door. He shook this off…but something was beating, very fast…no, it couldn't be…could his heart be…still beating? All this time? Whatever it was, he could feel it beating even faster knowing it was "there". He took another deep breath and grabbed the handle, twisted it…it was unlocked…he slowly pushed it open but then the door slammed back shut. This took Springtrap aback, this was something he wasn't expecting…the door was forced closed on the other side. He pushed the door again but to no avail, something was blocking the door. Springtrap grew annoyed and shoulder barged the door, it would open slightly but the force on the other side of it would keep it shut…each push and barged grew Springtrap from losing his temper.

His eyes started to glow angrily, he grunted and used all this strength and smashed the door open. The door swung and with a quick glimpse, he saw a figure scream and disappear…down some steps, the metal clanging sounded like it damaged this "thing" each time it got further down the steps. Springtrap for a second backed off but his curiosity got the best of him…he took a few steps forward and looked down the dark stairway…he couldn't see a thing…he then felt the wall, to find a switch of some sort.

Eventually he felt a square box attached to the wall and a switch, he clicked it and the light came on…but then started to flicker…dimly. Springtrap quickly thought that he was lucky to have lights on at all; especially of how run down it was…Springtrap, looked around and picked up a metal pipe that was randomly lying on the floor. He pulled it back, ready to take a swing at whatever it was he saw…and finally, he slowly went down the steps.

Thirteen steps were the space between the exit and whatever was down here. He casually carried on walking down the concrete steps…his breathing was starting to get heavy and his "heart" was beating much quicker now. He even took the time to gulp…

As he walked down, he could hear some sniffing and then a crying moan…his ears pricked up, they got louder and louder. The crying sounded like it was coming from a child…this freaked Springtrap a lot…but he had the pipe ready for any self-defence he had to use…he couldn't see a thing, even with his glowing eyes it didn't seem to improve his vision much…he stretched out his arm, waving it about, hoping to feel something. He managed to find a table next to a wall and began to feel the contents. The crying was nearer now…and sounds of shuffling.

Springtrap started to shake more now…but then he felt a long curvy object, heavy when he picked it up. It seemed to have a strange lump on it, a switch, perhaps…he pushed it and behold, the walls light up but only as a spotlight…he sighed in relief to know it was a torch he found. Without hesitation, he waved the torch around, trying to follow where the crying noises where coming from…the cries grew louder with moans and squeaking gasps. He pointed the torch towards that sound…and the spotlight revealed the appearance of a yellow figure, obviously run down and dirty…like him but more…slick, almost new looking…but still run down. The figure was huddled in the corner, scared of the light, scared of being found…its hands blocked its face.

FIGURE: N-Nooo…l-leave…m-mmeeeeee a-alone…

Springtrap gasped…this yellow figure could talk, he started to assess this mysterious thing and the spotlight from the touch started from the bottom of the figures feet…they looked like…chicken feet. Springtrap slowly moved the torch upwards…a slick smooth, but run down body, a feminine body… then the hands…one was missing but the other was trying to block the light…

FEMALE FIGURE: G-G-Gooooo aaaa-away…d-dooo-don't hurt m-meee…

SPRINGTRAP: I'm…I'm not going to hurt you…

The figure jolted into another huddle fetal position; trying not to look at the light…Springtrap couldn't make out its face, no matter what angle he tried. He gently put down the broken pipe, so not to make any loud noises…it clanged on the hard floor but not threating. Springtrap carefully took some steps closer but not enough to scare this helpless thing. The figure still had its face covered. Springtrap kneeled down so he could be the same level as the figure.

SPRINGTRAP: It's…it's okay…I don't mean no harm…

FEMALE FIGURE: Gooooo a-away…

SPRINGTRAP: Please…please trust me…

Suddenly, Springtrap's eyes raised, he formed a memory, a vision of what may have happened.

He was staring at a girl, in a cute yellow dress with pretty daisies on them and a perfect ponytail for her long blonde hair. She was crying and looking up to him…

Trust me…

But the vision quickly cut to a screaming, a girl being forced into a suit, blood squeezing out her eyes.

The vision was gone within a second. Springtrap shook his head, what did he see…was this a memory? Had this happened? His focus then drifted to the helpless figure in the corner of the room. She was still shaking and her face still hidden. Springtrap blinked…he wanted answers to what he saw…but this seemed more important.

SPRINGTRAP: I p-promise I won't hurt you…

The figure slowly turned its head, but only seeing one side of its face, it was certainly female, judging by the dirty pink highlights and rosy-looking cheeks.

FEMALE FIGURE: H-how…how can I trust you…?

SPRINGTRAP: You've…you've got no reason to trust me but why would I hurt you…?

The figure turned its head, Springtrap's hand was still shaking…he gasped, and he saw the rest of her face…one side seemed to be perfect, but the other side was ripped to shreds, her plastic coating was gone, only one good eye, the other missing but glowing a white dot…her mouth was black, with a twisted grin but her endo-skeleton jaw was downwards, indicating fear and sadness…she was an animatronic, she twisted her body to turn around, it was still a sight of beauty with her curves but worn and cracked. She saw his face of what looked like disgust and started to cry, her head in her hands…

FEMALE FIGURE: I'm…I-I'm hideous…I'm…u-uuugly…

SPRINGTRAP: (*getting to grips*) No, n-no you're not…really, you're not…I'm just…j-just shocked to see someone…a person…(*she carried on crying, black oil seeping through her fingers, he tried to change the subject*) Look, I-I'm sorry…why…why don't you tell me your name…do…do you have a name?

The female figure started to wipe her tears but smudged over her face, she started to sniff but stared down at the floor, trying to catch her breath through crying.

FEMALE FIGURE: I…I don't remember m-my name…my real name, but…I've b-been called…Chica, Toy Chica…

The name rang familiar to Springtrap, as he thought it was a lovely name…but then it accured to him that…he couldn't remember his…it was strange, he could remember what happened to his brother…but he couldn't even remember…his own identity…

CHAPTER IV

Springtrap stretched out his hand to Toy Chica, who was hesitant at first. She looked at his smile, though a little creepy, she figured it wasn't his fault to look that way, as his mouth lining was ripped and showing off the worn out, dirty teeth…at least his voice sounded sincere anyway. She half smiled back at him and accepted his hand. She used her good hand and Springtrap gently pulled her back up. Despite missing some of her face, or at least the outer layer…she…she wasn't half bad. Springtrap would understand if Chica was scared of him at first…his face was no better. But it wasn't his face she was thinking of:

His voice…his voice sounded very familiar to me. Like I heard it only yesterday. Wait, something is coming back to me though…a restaurant, a clean restaurant…it was…busy, full of children…happiness is the feeling I've got right now, the place was full of happy children and parents…wait, I…I remember…I was…I was at the party…where…I heard his…v-voice…"what's up, little girl…you look kinda sad…"

Odd memories were coming back to Springtrap as well. He couldn't help but wonder where who she was and whether he had known her before.

Wow…she's…b-beautiful, whatever she is. Wait, I do remember she's an animatronic from Freddy Fazbear. But…w-why is she alive…? Did she…did she have the same fate as me…

For a while they stared at each other, the silence wasn't quite awkward but neither of them knew what to say next. Springtrap started to rub the back of his head and Chica looked away shyly. Springtrap produced a nervous smile but Chica then tried to think about the small memory she had. Eventually, Springtrap broke the silence.

SPRINGTRAP: So…uh…Chica, how long have you been here?

CHICA: I…I don't remember…

SPRINGTRAP: Not even how you became a…animatronic.

CHICA: I honestly can't remember…but…

Chica trailed off as it sounded like she didn't want to finish of the sentence but Springtrap was far too curious to just let it go.

SPRINGTRAP: Yes…?

CHICA: I don't want to say…

SPRINGTRAP: Why?

CHICA: Because it sounds…stupid…

SPRINGTRAP: Chica, listen…none of this is making sense to me. I…I think I was human once and have faded memories...all I remember is…running scared. I'm confused Chica…I think I've…c-come back from the dead. (*chica gasped a little*) I need to know what you know…it's just weird that you're…like this…

CHICA: Ugly…?

SPRINGTRAP: No, that's not what I meant! I mean, you, now…like this…a robot, an animatronic. I mean, this can't be possible, right? Can it…?

CHICA: I guess so…

SPRINGTRAP: You guess so?! I don't understand what's going on here, Chica, it's also freaking me out that…"this" whatever "this" is, has happened to you. I believe we died and…and are paying for it…

CHICA: You mean, like a…sin? Our life in another time has caused this to be a form of…p-punishment…

SPRINGTRAP: I guess along those lines, yes.

CHICA: That's crazy…I…I don't recall…

SPRINGTRAP: Listen, I…did…something bad, something that'll haunt me forever. I only just got that memory back. I don't know why I did, but I did it…and if this is an act of God telling me that this is my punishment then fine. Maybe this is what hell is…but I still feel, like…I'm still alive…

CHICA: Then why should I be in the same hell as you? I…I…

SPRINGTRAP: You've got to remember something, Chica, you've got to!

CHICA: What does it matter?

SPRINGTRAP: Because I'm scared, Chica, I'm scared! I don't want to be…like this! Surely you must remember how you became like this!

CHICA: (*sighs a little*) I…only remember…

SPRINGTRAP: Yes?

CHICA: I remember…the screaming stopping…

SPRINGTRAP: (*waits for more information, but chica doesn't speak any further*) Wait, that's it? The screaming stopped, that's all you can remember?

CHICA: Yes, I'm afraid so.

Chica felt she didn't need to tell Springtrap what else she remembered, as it probably had no relevance to the situation, except maybe his voice. But until she could remember more, she stayed silent and kept her thoughts to herself.

SPRINGTRAP: This is…this is crazy. We're both animatronics and we have no idea why we're like this.

CHICA: Well, you said it's a form of punishment.

SPRINGTRAP: I don't know anymore…

Chica slowly got closer to Springtrap and gently touched his face, he looked her in the eyes and noticed her smile wasn't as creepy anymore.

CHICA: We'll find the answers. Don't worry…

Springtrap noticed a slight change in her personality, one minute she was scared out of her skin and now she's almost relaxed and confident. But it certainly didn't bother him much. It was nice to feel a warm hand over his face. He smiled back at Chica and then looked down at her handless arm…a sense of pity came across him.

SPRINGTRAP: How…how did you lose your hand?

CHICA: Oh…I just…fell…

SPRINGTRAP: You fell…?

CHICA: Yeah, it was silly of me. Of course I broke my hands with the fall, though as you can see, doing so snapped my hand right off. (Bits her lip) It hurt so much…

SPRINGTRAP: Yeah, I bet.

CHICA: But there was a cupcake attached to my hand-

Springtrap's eyes grew wide, within a second….a memory crept back in.

Yellow…daisy…dressed girl…showing me a cupcake…

"this is my cupcake, I won it!"

Cut to:-

"I…I lost my cupcake…"

Cut to:-

I…talk to her…

"hey, don't worry, little girl…I've got plenty of cupcakes. Do you want me to show you?"

"no, it's not a trick…"

"trust me…Leanne…"

But the vision quickly cut to a screaming, a girl being forced into a suit, blood squeezing out her eyes…skull cracks…

SPRINGTRAP**:** Oh, oh God…

CHICA**:** Is…everything okay?

Springtrap looked around him…it was like the memory took him to another place. He then looked at Chica who had a concerned face over her. Springtrap tool a small gulp and nodded his head.

SPRINGTRAP: Uh…yeah, I'm fine. Just had a…moment there…

CHICA: You seemed to have blanked out there

SPRINGTRAP: I guess I did for a minute there, yeah. (*Shakes his head*) Uh, sorry…you were talking about a…uh…a c-cupcake…?

CHICA: Well, yes, only the fact that I lost it when it broke as I landed on the floor. You can help me look for it if you want.

SPRINGTRAP: Um…s-sure.

Chica giggles and walks ahead of springtrap.

Isn't it obvious yet, you stupid lowlife scum? Can't you seeeeee? Can't you see it? You made her like this! Isn't it obvious?

Just then springtrap had another flashback memory.

A man in a near purple security suit was looking around at the children and the happy parents, he has never seen it this busy before, at least not since "the bite" that caused his own brother to be killed…thanks to him. But the party wasn't on his mind, he wanted satisfaction, he had a sick obsession…he couldn't control it, it consumed him…the fantasy to kill a human being…watching his brother's head crushed grew on him…the sounds…the screaming…

A little girl tugged on his shirt, he looked down and saw a little girl with blond hair in a ponytail, wearing a yellow dress with daisies on it, holding a cupcake and showing him it with pride.

"this is my cupcake, I won it!"

"that's great, kid, and good on ya"

She's perfect…

But just before he could say anything, she ran off into the busy crowd. He cursed that she ran off…normally children wouldn't come up to him, but this little girl was special and maybe a little to naive

Cut to:- sometime ahead, the little girl was crying. The purple man kneeled down to her, a little concerned.

"what's up, little girl…you look kinda sad…"

She sniffs. "I…I lost my cupcake…"

"lost…?" the purple man asks.

"yeah, some boys stole it…" said the little girl.

"those meanies…they should be taught a lesson, punished even…don't worry, kid, I'll teach them a lesson…"

The girl nodded but still the tears kept rolling down her cheek. The purple man pulled out a tissue and gently wiped the tears away from the little girl. He smiled back at her.

t worry, little girl…I've got plenty of cupcakes. ant me to show you? I've got loads out back…do you…do you want…one…?"

The girl's face brightens up and she smiles back at the purple man excitedly. The purple man gives his hand to the girl who takes it; he gently pulls the girl away from the crowd and party.

"do you really have a cupcake? Just one for me?" she asks

"I sure do" the purple man smiles

"this…I-isn't a trick, is it?"

"no, this isn't a trick. Say, what's your name, sweetheart?"

"…Leanne."

"trust me…Leanne. I have loads…"

Cut to: -

"I just…want to see your skull crush! I just want…to see how beautiful the blood creeps out of torn skin"

The girl is screaming as the purple man forces the little girl into a yellow chicken suit, the endoskeleton ripping through her skin, the force breaking her skull, the blood starts to flow from her eye sockets…blood filling up in her throat as she gurgles the blood out of her mouth. The bones snap and disjointed bones ripped through the skin…the neck snaps and then…the screaming stops and her body becomes limp…

"I CAN'T STOP BECAUSE THIS SATISFIES ME, IT SATISFIES ME!"

The memory ends.

Springtrap starts to feel like he's going to hyperventilate and he feels tight chested. Chica turns around and gasps at Springtrap's state…he just looks at her, his eyes wide open and fear surrounds him…not wanting to know the truth…

SPRINGTRAP: L-Leanne…? (*Chica's eyes go black*) You're…Leanne…I…I k-killed you…?

As Chica's eyes start to go black, she lets out a laugh, normal at first but then it becomes sadistic and almost glitchy, her voice loses its sweet innocence and becomes a voice of hell and groaning, almost echoing evil itself.

CHICA: Tttttttttttttheee…t-truth huuuuu-hhhurts, d-dooodoessss'nt it? Yoooooouuuu MURDERER! MMUUUUUUUR-MUURDERER!

Springtrap gasps as Toy Chica becomes nightmarish; he starts to turn to run but Chica grabs him in a flash and pushes him against the wall. He moans as he feels the force on his back and feels the tight grip on his neck. He starts to choke.

CHICA: Yoouuuuuuuurrrr t-tu-t-turn tooo s-suffer, noooooow! Your p-p-pai-PAIN-pain has ooooonly j-juuus-jus…just…B-BEGUN!

CHAPTER V

CHICA: Caaaaaaan yooou feel t-theeee pain? Caan you feeee-feeeel it?

Springtrap was finding it even harder to breath as Chica gripped on his neck tighter. He could feel his body getting weak. He tried to push Chica off him but she was incredibly strong. She chuckled at him with her raspy static voice and then chucked him across the room. He flew into a pipe, pretty much denting it and then fell hard on the floor…he felt pain, he couldn't believe he felt pain. He looked at the pipe he smashed into…a pipe leading from the ceiling and into a floor…steam was coming out of it. He looked back at Chica who was slowly and strangely seductively walking towards him and smiling. His confusion met with anger, his remorse was gone thanks to this animatronic trying to kill him…he grunted and got up. He then yanked at the pipe with all his strength but could only bend it slightly, making more steam come out.

CHICA: Yoooouuuu w-wiiil pay….

Springtrap noticed Chica was close. She then pulled back a fist, ready to punch him. Springtrap gasped and quickly dodged her punching attack, denting and snapping the pipe with a clean cut. He ducked as the steam blew into Chica's face. She screamed as the heat scolded her face and eyes, making her back off and covering her face with her one hand.

Springtrap took this opportunity to try and pull a piece of piping off, he did with ease…the steam died down and he gained a lead pipe, holding like you would with a baseball bat. Chica was still shaking violently over her painful face. She managed to look in the direction of Springtrap but he didn't give her time to react as he swung the heavy lead pipe across her face…the force twisting her face and almost snapping the connection to her neck. She fell awkwardly on the floor, her voice becoming a dying recorder and rasped her noises of pain.

CHICA: I'm…n-noooooott the o-ooo-onllly onne, you kiiiiled…aaaaaam-aaaam I?

Springtrap didn't want to answer as he raised the lead pipe over his hand and brought the metal weapon over Chica's head, instantly killing off her functions and herself. But Springtrap didn't stop, he continually smashed her head in over and over again, each force ripping a shred of plastic and metal off her face, each impact squashing and denting the metal endoskeleton. Springtrap carried on, he grunted and snorted at every movement, his arms starting to ache but he kept going…

Chica's head snapped off easily now and crushing up like an empty coke can. She was now nothing and Springtrap suddenly stopped. He just stared at Chica's lifeless body. He gasped and panted hard…he dropped the badly dented lead pipe, the sound clanking through the quiet room…he then fell to his knees and started to cry…his emotions were flying everywhere now.

SPRINGTRAP: I'm sorry…I'm truly sorry…if…if I could take it back, if I could go back in time and take it back, I would. I would! I FREAKING WOULD! If…I could go back and tell that stupid kid not to harm his brother, I would! That would've stopped my starting obsession of…k-killing. And p-poor Leanne, that poor g-gil…I took two lives…but I didn't care…I FREAKING DIDN'T CARE! BUT I DO NOW! I'M SOOOORRRY!

Worthless!
Scumbag!
Oxygen was wasted on you!

SPRINGTRAP: Get out of my head! GET OUT!

VOICE: Why? When you haven't learnt anything…

SPRINGTRAP: Now what? Who's there…?

VOICE 2: Can't you guess?

SPRINGTRAP: THIS ISN'T A GAME!

VOICE 3: You be right there, laddie…this isn't a game!

SPRINGTRAP: SHOW YOURSELF!

Just then a withered old Freddy, a faceless Bonnie and a torn up Foxy came out of the shadows, like they were part of the darkness. But this was the maintenance room, they've been there the whole time. Springtrap got up, quickly grabbing the dented pipe and backing away. Like Chica, their voices were static but easy to understand. Each had blood coming out of their eye sockets, while Bonnie seemed to have a rotten child's head where his face was meant to be…the child's head wasn't moving, just Bonnie's body and bits of the mechanics rotating around the rotten flesh of the child's head and the voice coming from the vocal box. Springtrap gasped at the sight of all three.

SPRINGTRAP: Oh God…

FREDDY: Threeeeee…more…

BONNIE: That makes…fiiiive…in t-toooo-tal…

FOXY: Yeeee killllled five….F-F-FIIIIIVE!

SPRINGTRAP: Five…?

FREDDY: Don't deny it! Don't DENY IT!

SPRINGTRAP: But I…I don't remember…

Just then he gasped, as the memories again came flooding back. They were quick, it was like watching a slideshow, a slideshow of horror.

-A young boy of about 9, wearing blue having his arm broken, a quick snap to an unnatural side so he could fit into a suit, a blue rabbit animatronic suit, the bone ripped through his flesh a stuck out…loud screaming…

-Cuts to another memory of a boy dressed as a pirate, his face being crushed by an endoskeleton, as a large adult hand forcefully pushes the poor boy against the metal…scream stops as the skull cracks and eyes roll back, almost falling out of the sockets…

-Cuts to the last memory…a boy being chased down a hallway…screaming, loud screaming of fear…

Gun…black handheld gun.

The gun gets cloaked, ready to fire…the boy dressed in a brown t-shirt is still running down the hallway…

BANG

The boy falls down…

Laughing is coming from the adult, the boy is crying in pain…blood pumping out of his bullet hole wound in his back. The boy begs, crying and in pain, tears streaming out of his eyes…

"I w-want my mommy…I…I want to see m-my d-d-daddy…"

Gun clocks.

"P-please…I…I'm s-scared…I…I don't want to die…"

The adult points the gun at the child's head, laughing.

*"MOMMY! DADDY! HELP M-**bang*

The head is ripped from the bullets impact and blood sprays everywhere as chunks of flesh and skull are splattered all over the floor, quickly flowing a pool of blood…

The memories fade…Springtrap starts crying. He cries into his hands as he drops the metal lead pipe again. It was all becoming clear. Suddenly, the voices coming from the animatronics were starting to clear up, for reasons unknown.

FREDDY: Five. You killed five! (LAUGHS) And your crying? To late!

BONNIE: Why should we pity you! When you stuffed us!

FOXY: We, the children, demand JUSTICE!

-So, what's gonna happen to him-

FREDDY: Justice!

BONNIE: Justice for us! Justice for the pain you brought upon us!

FOXY: You have yet to feel what we feel! Endless pain! Endless, endless pain!

Springtrap looks at up the withered animatronics, who were looking down at him. His tears still flowed out but he managed to stop crying…he gulps through the lump in his throat.

-I'm afraid there's nothing we can do for him. He's crazy.-

SPRINGTRAP: Do…do what you have to…I…deserve your…p-punishment…I'm…a monster…I deserve it

The animatronics smiled. Foxy kicked Springtrap in the face, Freddy repeatedly stamped on his chest and Bonnie turned and twisted each of his joints. Springtrap screamed, the pain was unbearable…snap of metal, snap of plastic…

-But without a doubt. He murdered those poor children…though his brother was an accident, it started an obsession. Yes, I'm afraid Vincent is going to be with us for quite some time…-

Then, just like that, the pain was gone…darkness…

EPILOGUE

There was a long corridor, all the walls were white but slightly worn and dirtied up. Along this corridor were loads of doors on the right and left of the room; they were in rows to the beginning and end of the long hallway. The floor was chequered in a black and white fashion that went along with the corridor – the only thing that was not making the room dull.

Footsteps then echoed the room, after a sound of a door opening. A middle age man, wearing a long white doctor's uniform was walking down the corridor, holding a clipboard. It was a few more seconds before he stopped and checked his clipboard, his eyes assessing the information he had in front of him. He then looked at the door number…87. He nodded and slowly approached the door…the door was heavy and made of thick steel. He pulled away the window flap and looked inside…

Just then, a door from the opposite end of the corridor opened and the doctor acknowledged this and saw a policeman approach him. The doctor nodded towards the policeman, who tipped his hat back as a form of hello. The policeman then looked through the small window flap in the door while putting his hands on his belt, relaxing his arms. They were both looking at a man who was sitting in the corner…he was in a fetal position but tied in a straight jacket and then he started screaming.

CRAZY MAN: SCREW YOU, YOU ANIMATRONICS.

POLICEMAN: (*sighs*) Any news? Any change?

DOCTOR: No, not what you already know.

POLICEMAN: Right. But I'll need to have an official confession even if it means beating it out of him.

DOCTOR: Do you really think that's necessary?

POLICEMAN: (*grunts*) I think for the poor families that lost their children to this monster, yes, it is necessary! A confession as soon as possible so we can hang this nutjob.

DOCTOR: Please be patient…we have a few tests to run on him first…

POLICEMAN: Tests? He doesn't need tests, look at him, he's a crazy shit. Does he still think he's a golden rabbit, eh?

DOCTOR: Yes…but I have to admit, he does have an interesting imagination. He believes he was killed in a "Springtrap" suit and that the souls of the children, he killed, came back to haunt him…30 years into the future.

POLICEMAN: (*shakes his head*) Crazy son of a bitch. He should be shot!

DOCTOR: Yes, I do agree but we need to analyse people like him to see what makes him tick. A case like this doesn't come often…

POLICEMAN: This is gonna be a long process, isn't it?

DOCTOR: I'm afraid so…

POLICEMAN: Those families demand justice.

DOCTOR: In time, in time…I promise they will.

POLICEMAN: (*sighs, with a slight pause*) So, what's gonna happen to him?

DOCTOR: I want to find out what's in that brain of his. Head scans, the currents in his brain…his mind…

POLICEMAN: I doubt you'll find anything…he's to far gone.

CRAZY MAN: SCREW YOU, SCREW YOU! YOU GOD DAMN CHICKEN! YOU PIECE OF SHIT, BEAR! BASTARD FOX! GODDAMN BUNNY! I'M SORRY!

POLICEMAN: (*frowns*) God…yeah, he's gone. Far to gone…way beyond.

DOCTOR: (*nods*) Yes. I'm afraid there's nothing we can do for him. He's crazy.

POLICEMAN: I could've told you that.

DOCTOR: Mmm. Beyond, like you said. But without a doubt, he murdered those poor children…though his brother was an accident, it started an obsession. Yes, I'm afraid Vincent is going to be with us for quite some time…and thanks to this gentleman they have closed

Freddy Fazbears for good, its reputation is long gone.

VINCENT: (*talking to the wall*) LEAVE ME ALONE. I'M SORRY!

The crazy man then started running into the padded walls as hard as he could and a few times he attempted to jump at the wall and fall hard on the ground, even if it was slightly padded.

VINCENT: (*Looks around confused as he gets up*) Wait! What is this place? Where am I? What the hell is this place? Where is my brother? It's his birthday today! I'm missing his birthday!

POLICEMAN: Stuffing kids in an animatronic. Sick bastard. He'll get the injection soon. Well, I guess I'll leave you to it, doctor. I'll be round again sometime next week, I suppose. Hopefully, you find what you're looking for.

DOCTOR: I'm sure we will, officer, I'm sure we will.

The police officer tipped his hat and walked away. The doctor carried on looking at Vincent and then quickly wrote on his clip board.

"Patient 87: Vincent purple. Former night guard.

Multiple split personalities. One strong personality that appears before us…is a persona called…Mike Schmidt, this side of him believes he died and awoke in the future…and also the responsibility of killing five children…that includes his brother and the way he took action for his murders

As Vincent he seems to have blanks in his memory, he only seems to recall his brother's birthday, though this is still to be questioned. This of course is still a real memory.

My verdict is that killing his brother started an obsession and he created Mike Schmidt that took over to blank his real mind of what he was up to. His persona took over and the killing spree began.

Vincent and mike are trapped in one body; they are pretty much…the same person"

Insane asylum.

-The End-

Made in the USA
San Bernardino, CA
17 November 2016